Mallory
The Forgetful Duck

Written by Elaine Allen
Illustrated by Kelli Nash

To Leo
Dy wishes from Mally!

E. Allen

Written by Elaine Allen

Illustrated by Kelli Nash

Mallory
The Forgetful Duck

Schiffer Publishing Ltd®

4880 Lower Valley Road • Atglen, PA • 19310

Other Schiffer Books by the Author:
Olly's Treasure, 978-0-7643-3772-7, $16.99
Olly the Oyster Cleans the Bay, 978-0-87033-603-4, $13.95

Other Schiffer Books on Related Subjects:
Osprey Adventure, 978-0-7643-3684-3, $13.99
Quiet Please—Eaglets Growing, 978-0-87033-541-9, $11.95

Text Copyright © 2012 by Elaine Allen
Illustrations Copyright © 2012 Kelli Nash

Library of Congress Control Number: 2011943318

Designed by Danielle D. Farmer
Cover Design by Bruce M. Waters
Type set in Ajile/Americana

ISBN: 978-0-7643-4069-7
Printed in China

Schiffer Books are available at special discounts for bulk purchases for sales promotions or premiums. Special editions, including personalized covers, corporate imprints, and excerpts can be created in large quantities for special needs. For more information contact the publisher:

Published by Schiffer Publishing Ltd.
4880 Lower Valley Road
Atglen, PA 19310
Phone: (610) 593-1777; Fax: (610) 593-2002
E-mail: Info@schifferbooks.com

For the largest selection of fine reference books on this and related subjects, please visit our website at www.schifferbooks.com
We are always looking for people to write books on new and related subjects. If you have an idea for a book, please contact us at the above address.

This book may be purchased from the publisher.
Include $5.00 for shipping.
Please try your bookstore first.
You may write for a free catalog.

In Europe, Schiffer books are distributed by
Bushwood Books
6 Marksbury Ave.
Kew Gardens
Surrey TW9 4JF England
Phone: 44 (0) 20 8392 8585; Fax: 44 (0) 20 8392 9876
E-mail: info@bushwoodbooks.co.uk
Website: www.bushwoodbooks.co.uk

Dedication

For my children Lindsey and Owen, who are without a doubt the most beautiful "ducklings" in the whole world. And to my husband Peter, for his loving support. –EA

To the Nash, Graham, and Taylor Families—who all love and enjoy their Chesapeake Bay adventures! Thanks to all by helping to keep our Bay clean for our wildlife to wander! –KN

ALONG the marshy shoreline of the Chesapeake Bay there lived a Mallard named Mallory, and she was very forgetful. At times, Mallory would forget whether she had eaten

her breakfast, or whether she had taken her
morning flight along the bay for her exercise.
Or, she would forget if she had taken her nap.
It was not unusual for Mallory to take several
naps a day.

ONE day as Mallory flew out along the bay for her morning exercise, she forgot where she had left her nest, and indeed where she had laid her eggs!

"Now where did I leave my nest?" she wondered aloud. She looked and looked, flying here and there, until finally she saw a nest sitting in a grassy meadow not far from the shore. The nest was made of grass and moss and lined with soft downy feathers. Five creamy white eggs nestled in the middle.

"There's my nest!" Mallory cried. And she swooped down to sit on top of her eggs.

BUT before Mallory had time to settle and get comfortable, a Canada Goose dove down and perched on the edge of the nest. "Excuse me!" honked the Canada Goose. "You are sitting on my eggs!"

"Good gracious!" cried Mallory, hopping off the nest. "I am sorry. I seem to have forgotten where I made my nest and laid my eggs. Are you sure these are your eggs?"

"Of course," snapped the Canada Goose as she pounced upon her nest and hugged her eggs.

"But how can you tell these eggs are yours?" Mallory wanted to know.

"Why it's easy," replied the Canada Goose. "I can see plainly that these are mine. Aren't they *the* finest eggs you've ever seen?"

"Oh yes," Mallory agreed. "They are quite lovely." Mallory reluctantly left the nest with the Canada Goose and flew up into the air.

"My eggs have to be here somewhere," she said as she fluttered about. Soon she spotted a nest on top of a channel marker. It was made of cornstalks and branches, and there in the middle of the lofty nest laid three pink eggs with brown spots.

"There's my nest," said Mallory and she swooshed over to sit on her eggs. "I am here," she told them. But before Mallory could snuggle down and create proper warmth for her eggs, an Osprey bounded into the nest and nearly knocked her over!

The Osprey dropped a large fish into the nest before shouting, "Get off my nest!"

"Your nest?" cried Mallory, "but these are my eggs."

"Of course they are not your eggs," chirped the Osprey loudly. "It is clear for anyone to see they belong to me. My eggs are the prettiest eggs you will find anywhere."

"Yes," Mallory agreed, "they are a wonderful shade of pink." Mallory left the nest quickly for the Osprey was about to push her off! "Quack, quack!" she yelled as she took flight once again and continued her search.

"Where oh where is my nest?" Mallory said to anyone who would hear. She worried that she may never find it. Soon Mallory flew over a wooded swamp, and there high up in a tree she caught sight of her nest. "I have found you at last!" she cried. Her nest was big and roomy and there amongst a bed of twigs and sticks rested four eggs the color of the sea. "Hello, eggs," she said happily.

BUT, before Mallory could get to know her offspring better, a large shadow passed over the nest and a Great Blue Heron landed beside her. The roomy nest now seemed very crowded.

"Can I help you?" Mallory asked the stranger.

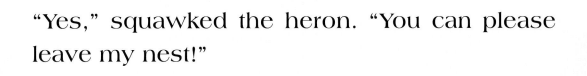

"Yes," squawked the heron. "You can please leave my nest!"

"Oh no!" cried Mallory. "Not again. But are you sure these are your eggs?" Mallory asked just in case.

"Why of course," the blue heron assured her. "I would know my eggs anywhere. My eggs are the most attractive eggs in the entire bay watershed."

"Yes, a very good size," Mallory agreed. She sadly left the Great Blue Heron behind.

"Now think very hard," Mallory told herself as she flew about once again. "Where would I have put my nest?" Before long she came across a shallow nest made of crushed shells on the sandy beach. Amongst the shell fragments sat three buff colored eggs with brown spots.

THE nest was smaller than the Great Blue Heron's nest. Much more her size. "Could these be mine?" Mallory wondered as she glided down to the nest. She looked all around her, but there were no other birds in sight. "You must be mine. I am sorry I was gone for so long," she told her eggs before plopping down and taking a much needed nap.

BUT Mallory was rudely awakened by a very noisy…*"Kleep! Kleep!"* It was an Oystercatcher! And she looked very angry.

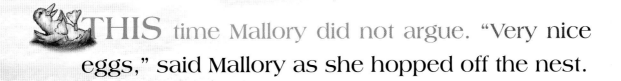 THIS time Mallory did not argue. "Very nice eggs," said Mallory as she hopped off the nest.

"The handsomest eggs in all the land," the Oystercatcher said smugly. Mallory agreed politely before flying up into the air once again.

"It's time to find my own nest and my own eggs," she told herself. Mallory felt very discouraged until she spied a familiar pond. She hurried down for a closer look, and there beneath the tall grasses she found her nest! Made of grass and leaves, it was lined with soft down. And all at once Mallory remembered that she had not yet laid her eggs!

WITH much relief, Mallory stepped gently into the nest and snuggled into its warmth. "Home," she said happily. Before long she laid ten light green eggs. But as Mallory sat on her offspring to keep them from the outside chill, she had a sudden fearful thought. "What if I forget!" she cried. "What if I forget about my eggs?"

MALLORY hopped off her nest and peered down at her newborns. As she gave each one a kiss she knew without a doubt that she would never forget, because her eggs were the most beautiful eggs in the whole world.

characters and humorous dialogue, magical events and cunning twists of plot, to name just a few.

The stories themselves are based on the realities as well as the mysteries of African life, both in the past and today. This is an innovative and unique collection that I greatly admire. I hope it will be welcomed by children and adults everywhere.

Vincent Magombe

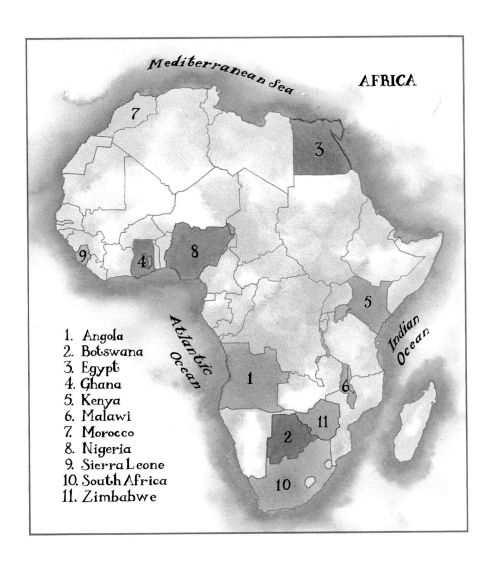

1. Angola
2. Botswana
3. Egypt
4. Ghana
5. Kenya
6. Malawi
7. Morocco
8. Nigeria
9. Sierra Leone
10. South Africa
11. Zimbabwe

THE RIVER THAT WENT TO THE SKY

Kasiya Makaka Phiri

A STORY FROM MALAWI

Once there was a River. It ran from one side of the great continent to the other, and it was so wide it looked like a lake, and the land around it was rich. All the animals that lived there had plenty of everything. Grass to graze, fruit to eat, nuts to crack, roots to chew, bark to nibble, and leaves to eat. The animals ambled all day long, eating a little, stopping, gazing into the distance, eating a little more, and going on slowly, for there was no hurry. The great vast River meandered across the land avoiding all the mountains, choosing only the plains and the valleys but always spreading wide, wide across the land. It rolled gently from one side of the vast continent and went to sleep and glided on the night tide to the other side. Backward and forward. It felt good and made happy noises on the banks, like the sound of calabashes filling with water, one gulp at a time.

On the banks grew the low grasses that like to trail their roots in cool river water. With them grew the papyrus and bulrushes. Behind them grew those grasses that like to smell the water every day and hear the happy sounds of the River. Water trees stood knee-deep in the water, looking toward the grasses of the low plains that gave way to ankle-high grass, then knee-high grass, all the way to the towering elephant grass. Then came the tall trees of the woods, beyond which were the high plains and foothills of great mountains. The high plains were covered in shorter grasses where the swift wind blew, keeping everything down except in the sheltered folds of the rolling ridges. In these hidden valleys were groves of rare trees and flowers and many other plants.

So everything was all right, until one day the River, gliding sleepily, looked up and saw the stars in the night sky.

"What is that?" said the River in a sleepy voice.

Hyena, who happened to be nearby taking a sip of water, looked up and said, "What's what, where?"

"Up there with the many eyes," said the sleepy River.

"That is the night sky," Hyena said and went on his way.

"Oh, how I wish I could go to the sky," said the River, sighing as it fell asleep.

The grass with the roots in the water heard this and whispered: "The River wants to go to the sky."

The whisper went on, to the papyrus, to the reeds, to the short plain grass, and to the knee-high grass.

"The River wants to go to the sky!"

"The River..."

"...wants to..."

"...go to..."

"...the sky...."

The whisper went very fast until it was at the edge of the woods that are hedged by bushes guarding the foothills of the great mountains and the high plains.

"The River wants to go to the sky," said a bush, and the trees whispered from trunk to branch to leaf to leaf to leaf like a gentle stir in an invisible breeze all the way to the wind-swept high plains where the grass lay low below the swift wind.

The wind was quick at picking up whispers from the lower plains, so it snapped the whisper up and dragged it over the high plains up to the mountains and over the peaks, where nothing grew because it was too cold. Away into the sky the wind carried the whisper.

"Shoosh-whoosh, whoosh-whoosh, the river wants to go to the sky."

The night sky heard it, the stars heard it, and early the following day before dawn, just as it was eating its breakfast ready to start the day, the Sun heard it.

"Very well, I'll visit the River today," said the Sun.

The River woke up very early, and soon after, the Sun came to visit.

"I hear you want to go to the sky, meandering River?" said the Sun.

"Yes! Oh, to walk the blue and see the twinkling eyes," the River sighed.

"Very well," said the Sun. "I can help you up but you'll have to find your way down."

"Down! It looks so beautiful up there, I won't want to find my way down."

Gazelle, who happened to be taking a drink just then, sprang up and ran to Elephant and said, "The Sun is going to take the great River up to the sky, and she says she'll never come back here again!"

Elephant thought for a while then raised her trunk and blew a message into the air. The wind, who was always quick at picking up messages, snapped it up, and everywhere it blew the animals and the plants heard it.

The trees were the first to react. They gathered together into the densest forest ever and talked over the matter for days and days. The gathering of trees and creepers became a jungle, but the grasses, thinking it was too dark under the eaves of those huge trees, wandered out onto the plains, and they were so happy they rocked in the wind singing in their throaty voices.

They spread as far as the eye could see. Some small thorn trees and bushes came out and dotted the grassy plains, and this became the savanna.

When the animals gathered they too talked for days and days.

"This is a serious matter," said Elephant.

"It is time to migrate to faraway places," said Rhino. Saying so, he put down his head and followed his nose South. South, South, always South. That started the exodus, and animals wandered in all directions. Great Gorilla and Brainy Chimpanzee, feeling that they did not want to go too far, simply went into the jungle. Tree Pangolin, Leopard, Gabon Viper, and Royal Antelope did the same.

Elephant led a whole delegation South following the rhinoceros. Buffalo, Lion, Giraffe, Gazelle, Hyena, Zebra, Cheetah, and many others wandered South and roamed the grasslands. But rock-climbing Barbary Sheep, Camel, Addax, Sand Cat, Desert Hedgehog, Fennec Fox, Jerboa, Sand Grouse, and many others remained exactly where they were.

Meanwhile, the Sun had gathered all its strength. It sent its hottest rays to heat the River, and slowly, oh so slowly you could not see what was happening, the River started to lift in particles too tiny for the eye to see. Up, up, up they went until they were so high that it felt cold. Then the tiny particles of the River huddled together and formed white fluffy clouds of all sizes. They were so happy to be floating in the air, and they waited in excitement for the spectacle of the night sky when they would walk among the many winking stars.

Sure enough, in the evening, the night sky prepared to lay out the best winking stars for the visiting clouds to walk among, and as it got darker the stars winked and twinkled and sparkled.

"Oh, isn't this wonderful!" said a cloud. "Simply stupendous!"

Whoosh! A gust of wind came in.

"You're sitting on my bit of sky ledge," the wind said.

"Oh, I beg your pardon," said the cloud, and she moved over to one side.

Whoosh! Gusts of wind came over and over again, here and everywhere. They claimed parts of the sky where the clouds were. Sometimes they came while the clouds were trying to get some sleep, and they would shake them awake and push them over.

Now, pushing and shoving is about the only thing that the gentle River would not stand. And all the clouds remembered the peaceful days of being water down on Earth. They remembered the gentle flow in one direction and the gliding back on the tide, and a small cloud said, "I want to go home."

Yes. They all wanted to go home. But how? The wind, so quick at picking up conversations, snapped up the news of the clouds trying to go home, and it gathered all its sisters, cousins, and brothers.

WWHHOOOSSSHH!!

They carried the clouds high and made them feel colder, and as the clouds huddled together they grew heavy and began to fall as rain. Down below, the Sun was still burning out any manner of moisture that remained in the river bed.

But it rained. It rained all day long and all night long. It rained everywhere but never in the old river bed. It rained in Abyssinia and formed the Blue Nile. It rained and rained and formed the White Nile and Lake Victoria and Lake Tanganyika and Lake Malawi and Lake Chad, Lake Turkana, and many small lakes besides. It rained and rained and formed the Shire River. It rained and formed the Zambezi. It rained some more and the Limpopo, the Orange, the Niger, the Luangwa, and many, many other rivers were born. It rained heavily and lightly, day and night, and if you put your hands over your ears and moved them on and off, you could hear something like a song but not quite a song. Something like words but not quite like words:

"I am the River, the River that went to the sky for a walk. I am the River, the River that went to the sky for a walk."

It rained and rained everywhere but never in the place where the River once lived. If any of the drops ventured anywhere near that place, the Sun bore down on them and sent them back into the sky. And it is true. If you go to the great continent of Africa today you will see the vast expanse of sand where the meandering River lived. Sand everywhere, even in places where grass had been plenty. To this day the wildebeest have not stopped running away from the Sun, following their noses to wetter places where the grass would be as it used to be once upon a time, a long time ago, on the great continent of Africa.

GONG GONG
Amoafi Kwapong

A STORY FROM GHANA

Kwaku Ananse is sometimes a man. Sometimes he is a spider. Among the Akan people of Ghana, everyone has heard of him. Kwaku Ananse is their folk hero.

He and his wife, Yaa Aso, are farmers, and they have four children. There are many, many stories told of Ananse and his family. Here is a story about Ntikuma, Ananse, and Aso's eldest son.

One fine day, Ntikuma was alone with his mother. His father, Kwaku Ananse, had taken the three younger children to the farm.

On this particular day, when Ntikuma was at home with his mother, he asked his mother for some money. He wanted to go to the market to spend it.

"Very well," said Aso. "You can have tuppence, but you must not forget to buy some black-eyed beans."

Ntikuma was pleased. Tuppence, which is the old form of two British pence, was a lot of money in those days. "I won't forget," said Ntikuma, and off he went to the market.

The market was busy and noisy. Everyone was either selling or buying. There was a lot of bargaining. There were fruit stalls full of coconuts,

Atea

Nkate

Adua

Atadwe

Paya

Akutu

Kokosi

borobe

Kwadu

Mango

Nkyene

pineapples, bananas, avocados, oranges, mangoes and so on. Other stalls had groundnuts, tigernuts, cashew nuts and so on. The women had clothes and cloth stalls. Ntikuma was on his way to the black-eyed bean stall. But suddenly, he heard a lovely rhythmic sound: GONG, GONG, GONG, GONG GONG. Ntikuma couldn't wait to get to the corner where the sound was coming from. He pushed his way through the crowd to see who it was making that lovely sound.

Ntikuma came to a big stall. The stall was piled high with drums of all shapes and sizes. There were tall drums and short drums. Square drums and round drums. And there were big drums and small drums too.

The man behind the stall was playing a Donno, which is a "talking" drum. GONG, GONG, GONG, GONG GONG.

So this is where the sound is coming from, thought Ntikuma, staring at the drums. He had forgotten all about the black-eyed beans. All he wanted was to buy the talking drum.

"How much is the Donno?" asked Ntikuma.

"Sixpence," said the man. Ntikuma held out his tuppenny piece. "This is all I've got," he said.

Ntaade

Ntama

Ntaade

"All right," said the man. "You look like an honest boy. You can have it for tuppence. But first, you must play me a rhythm."

Ntikuma put the Donno under his arm. He hit it gently with a curved stick. When he squeezed the strings around the drum, he got a higher pitched sound. He released the strings and the pitch sound was lower. Ntikuma made different sounds on the Donno. Suddenly, Ntikuma was able to play the rhythm he loved: GONG, GONG, GONG, GONG GONG. He loved it so much he didn't want to stop playing it.

Then suddenly, Ntikuma remembered the black-eyed beans. He had forgotten to buy any. "What will my mother say? What will she do? Now I am in big trouble." Ntikuma was so worried, he went round the market telling everyone what he had done. And he played his Donno as he spoke.

Aso akye me daama

"My mother has given me tuppence,
GONG, GONG, GONG, GONG GONG;

Ose memfa nkoto adua

She told me to buy some beans,
GONG, GONG, GONG, GONG GONG;

Mamfa akoto donno

I didn't buy beans,
GONG, GONG, GONG, GONG GONG;

Mede akoto donno

I've bought a drum instead.
GONG, GONG, GONG, GONG GONG;

Enne dee Aso aku me o

Mother will kill me
GONG, GONG, GONG, GONG GONG;

Enne dee Aso aku me.

She will be just mad with me.
GONG, GONG, GONG, GONG GONG."

The people at the market listened to Ntikuma. They liked the way he told his story. They all joined in with the rhythm – GONG, GONG, GONG, GONG GONG. They danced after Ntikuma as he went round the market. When Ntikuma set off home, the people followed him. They were still dancing. They even clapped and sang the rhythm.

Everyone was happy except Ntikuma. He didn't want to go home and

face his mother. He hated trouble. He started walking slowly. He was wondering what would happen.

Ntikuma arrived at his house. He stepped into the yard. And there was his mother dancing! Aso was dancing to the rhythm Ntikuma was playing.

"What a lovely rhythm!" said Aso. "Who made it up?"

Ntikuma smiled and told his mother all about the market. He told her about the Donno which made him forget the beans. He told her too about the rhythm and words. Aso didn't mind. She was proud of Ntikuma. She told him, "You are a very clever boy. You bought a drum which you can learn to play. The beans wouldn't last as long as the drum. Well done!"

All the people following Ntikuma came into the house. And it was quite a crowd! They had a great big party. The celebration continued through the night: GONG, GONG, GONG, GONG GONG. Later, Ananse and Ntikuma's younger brothers returned and joined in the celebration.

At cockcrow the people got ready to return to their homes. They knew that when the cock crows, "*Kokurokoo, ade akye o,*" it means, "Thank you for the memory, now morning has broken."

THE HUNTER AND THE DEER-WOMAN

Funmi Osoba

A STORY FROM NIGERIA

A hunter sat by a river to rest. He noticed a faint ripple in the water and when he looked closer, he saw that it was a woman bathing. The woman was as beautiful as sunrise. She had features so perfect that the hunter could not quite believe she was real. She was like a statue of a goddess. The sun shone on her rich brown skin. Her face radiated warmth and was as lovely as the drops of sunlight that were dancing on the water. She was the most beautiful woman he had ever seen.

The hunter held his breath and wondered who the woman was. She glided toward the bank, and the startled hunter slunk into the bushes. Then he saw a deer skin spread out on a low bush. It was the color of bronze and was dotted with dozens of spots as mysterious as cats' eyes. The hunter had seen many good animal skins in his time, but this was the most perfect of all. He reached out and sank his hands into its soft velvety folds. The hunter wondered how much such a fine skin would fetch in the market. More than two days' hunting, he thought, more even than a week's hunting, perhaps even as much as a month's hunting.

The woman swam up to the bank and climbed out of the water. She sprinted lightly across the soft grass toward him. The hunter rose in confusion. She stopped and stared at him. Her eyes were strange, like polished stone, but deep within them a bright spark of light flickered. The hunter stared at the woman, and for the first time in his life could think of nothing to say. The woman looked curiously at the hunter and reached out for the skin, silently imploring him to release it.

Then the hunter knew who she was: a deer-woman, one of the clan of the deer people. He had heard of these mysterious creatures who were rumored to roam the ancient forests. Half beast, half human, they could change into either creature at will.

He handed the woman back her skin, but as he watched her walk away he felt as if someone was tearing out his heart. He felt such an overwhelming sense of loss that he cried out, "Wait! Please!"

The deer-woman stopped and looked round. The hunter rushed up and kneeling before her, he begged her to marry him.

"But, dear man, you are a stranger," the deer-woman replied in astonishment.

"Yes, but a stranger who loves you more than life itself," cried the hunter desperately.

The deer-woman looked curiously at this peculiar human. In his eyes she saw the love of which he spoke. She looked at him for a long time and then she said, "Promise me one thing. Promise me that you will never tell any human person the truth about me, for if you do I will leave and never return. Promise me this and I will come with you."

The hunter happily promised to keep the deer-woman's secret, and together they made the long journey back to the hunter's town.

Bliss, perfect bliss reigned in the hunter's home. For a while, two happier people would have been hard to find. The hunter kept his promise. He told no one where his wife really came from. People were curious, as they often are. The hunter told those who asked simply that his wife came from a distant village, and he told them in a voice that suggested they mind their own business. Most people left well enough alone. The two could have been happy for ever, for every day their love grew deeper and deeper. Oh, how it makes my heart sad to tell you what happened next. But tell I must.

Often happiness blinds us to the evil that sneaks about us like a thief at night. These two in their joy did not see nor hear the nagging tongues, the spiteful whispers, and the wicked eyes. Jealousy hung in the air like a stale smell. They did not see the evil in the two people closest to them.

The hunter's sisters were as ugly as the deer-woman was beautiful. They hated to see happiness, even their own brother, for it tore into them like a dagger stuck in their hearts.

The wicked sisters would not stop talking about the mysterious woman their brother had married. Where had she come from, they wondered. Who was she? Why had not one of her relatives come to her wedding? Why was she always so secretive and so vague when asked about her past? Could it

be she had something to hide? And her eyes. They wondered at those eyes. Strange eyes, hardly human. Yes, hardly human, they agreed, nodding as one. The seed of an idea began to grow. Could it be, they wondered, bristling with spiteful excitement, that she was not a human person after all? They too had heard the stories of mysterious animal people who roamed deep in the forests. They wondered and they wondered, and finally they came up with an evil plan.

The hunter no longer went off on long trips because he hated to leave his bride alone. But now the two evil sisters begged him to go off hunting. They told him that a wicked money lender would throw them out of their homes if they did not come up with money to pay him soon. They wept loud insincere tears and the deer-woman's heart melted. She gently urged the hunter to go. He must save his dear sisters from trouble.

The sisters smiled with evil glee when the hunter agreed with his wife. He picked up his bow and arrows, his hunting knife and bag, kissed his beloved wife, mounted his horse, and rode off into the forest.

The wicked sisters waited to put the next part of their plan into action. They knew what they had to find. So they waited and they watched.

One fine day, the deer-woman took her basket and headed for the market. The two wicked sisters saw her go: now was their opportunity. They crept up to the house, climbed in through a window, and began to search. They looked under tables and chairs. They searched the cooking place and stuck their heads in every pot in the house. They rummaged through drawers and shelves and every possible place.

They searched until they were tired and still they searched some more. Finally, thoroughly exhausted, they collapsed onto the floor. Just then, a startling sound caught their attention. They both looked up and saw that a bird was trapped in the rafters of the roof. It was fluttering its wings noisily.

An idea flashed in one evil sister's mind. She turned to look at her sister and slowly the idea transferred into her mind. The two climbed up into the rafters, and it wasn't long before they found the deer skin.

"All her airs and graces and she wasn't even human," sniffed one sister.

"Wait until the others hear about this," exclaimed the other triumphantly, already on her way down. They scurried out of the house like two thieving rats and just managed to disappear round the corner as the deer-woman arrived home.

With the deer-woman's secret discovered, the sisters set about making sure that the entire town knew of it. They spread the news in excited whispers to people who took those whispers to others. And so it spread like wildfire. Soon, the town was ablaze with the news. Everywhere wagging tongues told the story and itching ears listened.

Now the deer-woman could not go out without meeting sniggers and stares. Children followed her everywhere singing, "Deer-woman, deer-woman, show us your skin." Others shouted out names that were so cruel they are best not repeated.

The deer-woman wept and wept. Finally, she could bear it no longer. She got her deer skin down from the rafters and became a deer once more.

She walked into the forest and disappeared, never to return.

Meanwhile, the hunter returned to town and rushed straight home to see his beloved wife. He had missed her terribly. As he called out her name, the little bird still trapped in the rafters told him what had happened. The hunter set the bird free. He didn't care about punishing his sisters for what they had done. He knew he had to return to the forest to search for his beloved.

For seven years he searched in vain. He walked to the ends of the Earth and back. He grew weak and tired and hopelessly ill.

Finally, when he knew he could walk no farther, he returned to the river where he had first met the deer-woman and sat against a boulder. His heart was broken and he knew the end was near. He decided to remain by the river until death carried him to the great beyond. His eyes grew heavy and he fell into a deep, deep sleep from which he resolved never to awaken.

High up in a tree, a little bird was watching. The hunter had been kind to him once by letting him out of the rafters. To return the kindness, the little bird called out to all his friends and told them to search for the deer-woman.

As the hunter was taking his last breath of life, the bushes were parted by a beautiful deer, a deer with a bronze-colored coat that was dotted with dozens of spots as mysterious as cats' eyes.

The creature gazed at the sleeping man for a long, long time. Then, as the sun began to sink in the horizon, painting the sky orange, the deer came forward and nuzzled his face. The hunter awoke and found himself staring deep into eyes glazed like polished stone, with flickering sparks of light deep within them. Then a magical thing happened. The hunter began to shed his human skin. Underneath was a deer, as handsome as any deer that ever walked the Earth. As he stood, he kicked his hooves and shook his head. The two creatures nuzzled each other, telling in their secret language of love and longing. Together at last, they wandered into the woods.

It is rumored that there they still roam. Legend tells that on certain days, they return to the river where they first met, to cast off their deer skins and bathe together.

TWO OF A KIND
Masée Touré

A STORY FROM SIERRA LEONE

In the village of Makabai, the women spent most of their time buying and selling foodstuffs in the market. The men worked hard on their farms.

On the one side of the market there was a cookery shop. The owner of the cookery shop was called Yeabou, and she was a very good cook. Pa Foday Bangura, the Alpha of Makabai, was one of Yeabou's many customers. He always had breakfast at the cookery shop.

Everyone in the village tried to practice what Pa Foday had taught them about respect, love, and charity. Well, not quite everyone. There were two people who did not care about what the priest had to say. One of them was Luseni, Yeabou's husband. The other was Santigie, the brother of the village schoolmaster.

Luseni believed that wealth was a result of hard work and should not be shared. He counted every penny he earned from his farm, over and over again. He was so greedy that even the fruit flies kept off his farm produce.

Santigie was a good-looking man and was always well-dressed, but he was lazy. He never gave anything to anybody, but he loved to receive things from people and was always asking for gifts.

One morning after taking his breakfast, Pa Foday was sitting quietly on a

wooden bench enjoying the noisy but pleasant atmosphere in the market, when in the distance he saw a young man in a blue kaftan. Pa Foday was surprised to see such a well-dressed man going to the market. He called Yeabou out of her shop and said, "Tell me, Yeabou, who is that man?"

"Don't you recognize him?" said Yeabou. "It's Santigie. Who else would go around dressed up like he was going to marry a princess?"

Pa Foday watched as the figure in the blue kaftan walked toward the cookery shop. Santigie was feeling so hungry that his stomach was beginning to grumble. He sniffed the sweet smell of foofoo and okra sauce, which

Yeabou had just served to her husband, Luseni. Pa Foday watched as Santigie walked straight past and went into the cookery shop. Yeabou followed him back inside.

As soon as he entered the shop, Santigie got down on his knees. "Please, Luseni, give me some food and I will leave you in peace," he pleaded.

"Beg, beg, beg," replied Luseni. "Can't you do something to earn a living?"

"Of course I can," said Santigie. "I can beg."

Luseni turned his head away in disgust but Yeabou looked at Santigie with pity. "You can have some food for five shillings," she said.

Santigie ignored her. With shaking hands, he grabbed Luseni's feet dramatically. "Don't do this to me, Luseni, please! Give me some food."

Yeabou could stand it no longer. She dished out some foofoo and sauce for Santigie. He ate it gluttonously. When he had finished, he went out of the shop. He did not even look at Pa Foday as he went away. But Pa Foday had been watching, and when Yeabou came to the door of the shop, he called to her again.

"Has Santigie ever done a day's work in his life?" he asked.

"He doesn't see why he should," replied Yeabou. "You teach us to share and take care of one another, therefore Santigie believes that the whole village should take care of him. If we let him, he would even take away the air that we breathe for himself."

Pa Foday knew that Yeabou was right. He sighed. Standing up, he arranged his kaftan and said goodbye to Yeabou. "It is very difficult to say what is good and what is bad," he said. "Never mind, perhaps Luseni and Santigie will solve the riddle for us one day."

As he walked away, Pa Foday did not know how quickly his words would come true.

A few weeks later, the whole village was hit by famine. Luseni decided to move farther inland and set up house by a stream. He was pleased with himself. He was far from the bothersome villagers and his farm flourished. He built himself a barn where he stored his grain and the food he had bought on one of his rare journeys to the provincial town of Makeni.

But Luseni's happiness was soon cut short. Santigie often thought of Luseni and Yeabou, and he asked whether anyone knew where they had moved to. As Santigie was hardly anyone's favorite, no one bothered to help him. But one day, Santigie was trekking to the neighboring town of Kamaranka when he noticed a flourishing rice and vegetable patch along a river bed. Who on earth has got such green fingers, wondered Santigie. Suddenly he had an idea. Could it possibly be that old miser, Luseni? Santigie found a winding path and eagerly began walking along it, certain he would get a good meal at the end of it.

Santigie was right. He had indeed found the home of Luseni and Yeabou. Luseni himself had been looking out of the window of his house at the very moment that Santigie had appeared on the path. Luseni had to think fast. The last person he wanted to see was Santigie. He hurriedly asked Yeabou to wrap him in a black and white country cloth as if he were dead.

"What on earth for?" asked Yeabou in amazement.

"Because I am not prepared to share my food with Santigie. He is walking toward the house at this very moment. I know he's after my bushels of rice and would want some of the beans we have prepared. If he finds me dead he will be forced to return to town immediately to report my death and we will then have time to hide everything."

"Wait a minute!" snapped Yeabou. "Are you so greedy that you would pretend to be dead?"

"Do what I say, woman. He is probably outside the door by now."

Yeabou had no choice. As she tucked in the ends of the country cloth around Luseni's body, Santigie arrived.

"Knock, knock—anybody home?"

Yeabou, who had been taught some acting at the traditional Bundo

School, quickly rubbed some ash on her face and walked like a zombie toward the door, tears streaming down her cheeks.

Santigie was shocked. "Lord have mercy!" he cried. "What has happened to you?"

Yeabou could not control her tears. "Luseni is dead." Her voice choked as she said those painful words. "He died about an hour ago."

Santigie, although he was a lazy beggar, was nevertheless kindhearted. "How terrible to die here in the middle of nowhere," he said as he walked into the house. He looked at the still body on the sofa and thought, "Why work so hard, saving every penny, spending nothing on yourself, only to die at such a young age?" His eyes strayed around the room and rested squarely on the table that had been set for lunch. Then he noticed something. Yeabou was wearing a colorful boubou. A woman who had suddenly lost her husband would immediately put on a black boubou and would cover her face. "I don't like the look of this," whispered Santigie to himself.

"Could you kindly go back to Makabai and announce Luseni's death." said Yeabou, jolting Santigie from his thoughts.

"I cannot go on an empty stomach," he said. "Let me have some beans and then I will be fit for the journey. Right now my limbs are weak and my body feels numb from the shock of this news."

Luseni, on hearing these words, stirred inside his cloth covering and nearly screamed. Yeabou did not know what to say.

"Let me see my poor friend who has slipped away from the fruitfulness of this life," said Santigie.

"Please," said Yeabou, "it will soon be evening and the village crier should receive the news before three o'clock."

"Well, the best thing to do would be to dig a grave now, so that when the elders get here everything is ready," said Santigie with a twitch of a smile.

"It is not necessary," pleaded Yeabou. "There are people who can dig one in five minutes."

"You may have a point there," said Santigie, "but I could at least carry the body outside." He tied the ends of the country cloth, shook the body and dragged it outside.

By this time, Santigie was no longer interested in a free meal. He felt sick inside. How could a man stoop so low that he would pretend to be dead?

"Give me a spade," he said to Yeabou. "I really think Luseni should be buried right now."

"Wait!" shouted Yeabou. She didn't know what to do. If she insisted that Luseni stay in the house, she would have to go through seven days of cleansing and fasting and she was certainly not prepared to do that for the sake of her husband's greed.

Without waiting for Yeabou to answer, Santigie walked to the house, found a spade and began to dig the grave. By the time he was halfway through, Luseni was sweating with discomfort in his tightly wrapped cloth.

Finally, Santigie spoke to Luseni. "Now look, you miserable man, you listen to me. I am going to bury you alive if you don't agree to share your stock of grains and vegetables with me."

There was a short silence and than a muffled and embarrassed-sounding voice said, "Why should I? You will never be satisfied anyway. You will always beg—my grain and vegetables will not make any difference."

"Very well," said Santigie, "I will bury you alive. It will not make any difference. If you are alive you will continue to be greedy, causing pain to those who have nothing. Once you are buried, the world will be rid of you."

Santigie then grabbed the knotted part of the country cloth and pushed Luseni into the hole. Yeabou was horrified and fled to her room. As Santigie began to lift the earth with his shovel, Luseni shouted, "Let me out of here! You can have the grain, the goats, the house, everything, just get me out!"

Santigie paused, spade in hand. "I don't need your house," he said proudly. "I don't need anything. I know now that I can actually dig the soil like you, and have self-respect." He untied the knotted country cloth and released Luseni, who by then was soaked with sweat and red in the face.

"Oh, my friend," said Luseni with shame and regret. "You have taught me such a valuable lesson. Let's have a meal together."

NO PROBLEM
Asenath Bole Odaga
A STORY FROM KENYA

One morning, the House Fly tied a banana rope around her waist. She then left home. She was going out to the bush to collect some firewood. On her way, she met the Rock Lizard. The Rock Lizard had just been taking a bath and was lying on a rock, warming himself.

"How strikingly handsome you are, Rock Lizard!" began the House Fly. "I admire the beauty of your dark skin, for it glows, sparkles, and shines. It's incredible! You are truly good-looking!"

The House Fly went on praising the Rock Lizard's good looks. And she meant it because, as we all know, the House Fly is a creature with a good, open heart. And that is why she visits everybody and everything, in all sorts of places, whenever she likes.

The Rock Lizard didn't like it. He was a vain, stupid, suspicious fellow. He felt that such open admiration from the House Fly might bring him bad luck or somehow affect his good looks. So he rushed to get away from the House Fly's admiring eyes. Unfortunately, in his eagerness to escape he found himself in the home of Apol, the Water Buck's cousin.

Now Apol was a strict fellow. He immediately felt offended when the Rock Lizard came in. He objected and complained strongly. But he was not

satisfied with that. He thought he must register his complaint before an audience. For this reason, he called an urgent meeting of all the creatures of the wild. The move caused a real stir in the jungle. Each creature was anxious to find out why Apol had called such an urgent meeting.

As soon as he received the message, Elephant hurriedly left home and headed toward the place where the meeting was to be held. By bad luck, he did not take enough care or take account of his size. He just walked carelessly and hurriedly along the crowded road. In his hurry he stepped on the back of the Tortoise. At that time, Tortoise was the carrier of fire, and in his great fury and pain, the Tortoise let out some of that fire through his bottom. The fire leaped and licked everything that lay in its path. It even burned part of the Chief's house!

Now it happened that, at that moment, the Black Ant was airing her eggs on the roof of the Chief's house. As soon as the rain saw the Chief's house on fire, it came down in a big storm. It had to put out the fire in order to save the Chief's house. Unfortunately, it also washed away Black Ant's eggs, and the water carried them all into the lake. By then, all the creatures of the wild had gathered. They all came to attend the urgent meeting called by Apol, the Water Buck's cousin.

Black Ant was furious. It had taken her ages to lay the eggs. She called out to the rain, demanding: "Rain, why did you wash away my eggs? You have killed all my little ones! Please explain why you came down at the wrong time?"

"Oh, I am sorry, but what could I do?" replied the Rain. "When I saw the

Chief's house burning, I surely had to do something about the fire."

"That sounds interesting," the Chief remarked. "House, why were you burning?"

"I am sorry, sir," the House replied. "What could I do? Tortoise just let out the fire which was burning all the grass and trees around me. Fire is merciless. We animals can't control it. It must be taken away from us. Only Straight Ones, the human beings, are able to look after it." By now, the House was in tears.

"Tortoise, my old friend, what happened?" the Chief demanded. "Why did you let the fire loose? You know how destructive and uncontrollable it is!"

Tortoise turned his head with difficulty. He was still feeling much pain from his back where the Elephant had stepped on him with his huge legs.

"I couldn't help it," Tortoise lamented. "The Elephant stepped on my back. In fact, he's ruined me. My appearance is gone for ever. I'll never be my old self again. My coat is cracked and broken all over."

The other creatures showed great sympathy for the Tortoise.

"Please sit," the Tortoise said to the Chief. "I can no longer look after the fire. As the House has said, let's give it to the Straight Ones. They will now have to control it."

"We will see to that later," the Chief replied, turning to the Elephant. The Chief was very angry. "Elephant, why on earth didn't you look carefully before you stepped on the path? Your size doesn't give you the right of way in the jungle. I am the Chief, and I have given the right of way to every creature in the wild."

All the creatures nodded in agreement. The big fellows in the jungle had to take more care so as to safeguard the lives of the small ones.

"Oh, I'm very sorry indeed," Elephant said sadly, "but what could I do? I had to hurry to be here in time for Apol's meeting. His shouts and howls meant there was something urgent and he needed all of us. The jungle is full of danger. You have to hurry when one of us calls a meeting."

"Apol," the Chief called loudly. "Why did you call an urgent meeting of all the creatures of the wild? Why didn't you come through me? I am the Chief of the Jungle! What was the urgency?"

"I had to, because Rock Lizard invaded my privacy," Apol shouted, shaking with rage. "He just glided into my home where I live with my entire family. I had to demonstrate my full objection. This is a serious matter. He was breaking the law of my right to privacy."

The Chief cocked his head and looked hard at Rock Lizard. In a thunderous voice, he asked, "Rock Lizard, please explain why you intruded into Apol's home without permission? Quickly! Explain!"

"O Jungle Chief, strong and mighty," Rock Lizard replied haughtily. "What could I do when the House Fly so openly gloated on my beauty?" He looked around slowly at the creatures of the wild. It seemed as if he was advertising, showing off his handsomeness. He began again after a little pause. "How could I tell what her motives were? Or what she might do to me? Actually, I was horrified and scared stiff."

"Scared?" said the Chief. "What was it that scared you?"

"Chief, I have never before met a House Fly with a rope around her waist. So I thought that I was probably seeing a ghost or another strange sort of creature. Perhaps from another world! She looked funny."

The animals looked at the House Fly. She was still wearing a strong rope around her waist. They were very amused at the sight. And they began to laugh. All the creatures of the wild began laughing and they laughed long and hilariously. The laughter was utterly deafening. It was like many thunders rolled into one thunder. The House Fly laughed too until tears ran down her cheeks, and even the Chief couldn't hide his amusement.

When the great laughter died down, the Chief spoke to the House Fly. "House Fly, why did you so openly stare at

Rock Lizard and go on about his good looks?"

"Mmmmmm," the House Fly exclaimed, looking seriously at the Chief and all the other jungle creatures. "I am the House Fly, the daughter of the small ones who never live to see old age! What crime did I commit? I had no ill feelings toward Rock Lizard. I only stopped to admire the good looks of the beautiful one. Was that serious enough to trigger off such a chain of events?"

The House Fly looked mischievously at the Rock Lizard. "Chief of the Jungle, great and mighty leader of us all, look at me," she said. "I'm small and insignificant. I am deprived of good looks. But I am free to look and admire. So if the good-looking members of the wild display themselves, then it's only natural that I should gaze at them. Please assist such members to find an answer to their problems. I myself have none. I have no problem." And the House Fly flew away singing loudly.

A MOST FAMOUS BAKER

Eva Dadrian

A STORY FROM EGYPT

One, two, three... the white bread rolls in the tall box. One, two, three, four... the brown round loaves on the wooden tray.... Half asleep, Samir was running his hands from one tray to the other. One, two, three, four... one more row and he would move to a new box.

It was four o'clock in the morning. Samir had promised his uncle that the boxes would be ready on time but the young boy was feeling tired. He could hardly open his eyes. Usually, he did not need to. After six months of apprenticeship, Samir had learned that his uncle used the right-hand oven to bake the white bread and the left-hand oven to bake the brown bread. He also knew exactly how far he had to stretch his arm to pick up the bread from the tray and place it inside the box. But today was a completely different day, and he was not allowed any mistakes.

Uncle Fathi was no ordinary man. He was a Master Baker. His bread was the best in town, and people came from far away to buy his crisp, piping hot, freshly baked loaves.

Samir liked working for Uncle Fathi. Early in the morning when the delivery boys had left, uncle and nephew would go upstairs to the kitchen to have their first meal of the day. Because Uncle Fathi had never gone to

school, he could not read or write, and Samir made a habit of reading the newspaper to him every morning. Samir enjoyed these rare moments when he was alone with his uncle and there were no more breads to count or boxes to fill. For almost an hour he would read the newspaper while his uncle prepared the food.

After reading the front page articles, Samir would then choose something light and funny from the gossip columns. He knew how much his uncle liked to laugh about actors and television personalities. In the meantime, Fathi would take out from the stove a pot of broad beans, and smashing the beans in a large plate, he would mix them with plenty of pure olive oil, lemon juice, and cumin. Sometimes he would also slice a tomato or chop some fresh green spring onions. Served with hard-boiled eggs, a large pot of tea, and of course some freshly baked bread, there was nothing better.

"Come on, son," his uncle would call. "It's breakfast time."

Samir would then stop reading, fold the newspaper, and move his chair nearer to the table. Pulling his sleeves up to his elbows, he would dip his bread into the delicious juices of the broad beans. Every single bite was a real joy. "Today, it's excellent," he would admit, "it's even better than yesterday," and his uncle would reply that the goodness was not in the beans but in the bread.

Samir sighed, his mouth watering at the thought. There would be no break for beans this morning. He had filled more boxes than usual already and more were still waiting. Samir continued his counting. One, two, three, four.

All this great fuss had started yesterday. Uncle Fathi and Samir had just finished their breakfast and were coming downstairs to serve their morning customers. Waiting on the sidewalk outside were two gentlemen dressed in dark suits. The men explained that they were from an American company which owned three hotels in Cairo. They produced business cards and handed Uncle Fathi a document to read and sign. Without revealing that he could not read, Fathi asked Samir to study the paper. It was a two-year contract to supply all the bread that their hotels in Cairo needed, beginning the next day!

What an honor for my uncle, thought Samir turning to him, but Fathi was already inside the bakery. There was no time to lose. The doors of the bakery were shut and Uncle Fathi moved to the back room to start preparing the bread.

"The secret lies in the mixing," he said to Samir as usual, as he measured out his best flour, and added water and yeast. But if ever there was any secret, it was in the way Fathi worked the dough. All that day and all that night, Samir worked by his side, watching as the dough became as light as a feather. When it was ready, Uncle Fathi stood up, stretched his arms, and

went to wash his hands. When he came back, he said his prayers, lit the ovens, and baked the most wonderful bread he had ever made.

As dawn was breaking, a tremor shook the bakery. A big white truck turned into the narrow street. All the surrounding buildings vibrated as if there was an earthquake, and the entire neighborhood woke up. People came out of their houses anxiously looking at each other. It was the first time that such a large vehicle had ever come into their street, and at such an early hour.

Samir opened wide the doors of the bakery, and four young men dressed in navy-blue overalls jumped from the back of the truck. In less than an hour

the work of a whole day disappeared into the back of the truck. When they had finished, the driver locked the back doors, signed the receipt prepared by Samir, and went off in a cloud of dust.

As soon as the truck left, the neighbors began asking questions. Uncle Fathi, who had been on his feet for the past twenty-four hours, sat down at his counter and explained everything. He explained how he got the special new contract, how he and Samir had worked all day and all night, and how proud he was of his young nephew who had helped him so much.

Samir was also proud to be part of his uncle's new success. He had forgotten how tired he felt just half an hour ago.

The next day, Uncle Fathi received a visit. A local journalist had heard about his neighbor's good fortune while having breakfast at Hagg Youssef's coffee shop, which was next door to the bakery. An article with Fathi's picture was quickly published in the local newspaper, reporting the baker's great success. Soon dozens of other journalists besieged the bakery. They transformed Fathi into a national hero and splashed his picture all over the newspapers.

The next day, busloads of new customers came. Everyone wanted to taste the bread from the bakery that supplied the big American hotels. Women arrived in groups of ten, with screaming children in tow. Men drove from their offices in brand-new cars to buy Fathi's "unique" bread, as the newspaper called it. Hagg Youssef, the coffee-shop owner, decided to supply tea and coffee. Sandwiches were made outside on the sidewalk. Soon it was impossible to move in the narrow street. Everywhere, people were eating and drinking, and before long, scraps of food left all over the sidewalk attracted hundreds of flies.

It was chaotic. Things were bad enough already with all the people. Now there was an army of flies, and poor Uncle Fathi did not know what to do to protect his bread. They were flying and buzzing all over the place and would not go away. Uncle and nephew chased them in vain, cursing them while swatting them in their hundreds.

There was no end to the invasion. While Uncle Fathi was chasing them

across the bakery, Samir pursued one particular fly right outside the shop. The fly went around and around and sat on the nose of the barber's wife. In his rush to kill it, Samir raised his arm and Squasshh!!!—he swatted the fly on the very nose of the poor woman. Screaming and cursing him she ran off holding her nose. Everyone laughed except the barber. He was not amused. Not at all.

"I'll tell your precious hotel owners all about you," he yelled. "I'll tell them all about your filthy, full-of-flies bakery!"

He said he would ask them to come and see for themselves.

This was a real catastrophe. Uncle Fathi did not know what to do. He knew that in a day or two, when everything calmed down, the flies would be sure to go away. But in the meantime, his whole reputation was at stake, and he could not allow his big contract to be canceled in this silly way.

Something had to be done and fast, before the barber decided to fulfill his promise and telephone the hotel. Samir tried to explain that he did not mean to hurt the lady, that it was a complete accident which he regretted greatly. He did not get very far. Everybody was talking at once, children were roaring around the sidewalk, and dogs were barking all over the place.

Suddenly Hagg Yousseff, the coffee-shop owner, came up with a wonderful idea.

Later that evening, Samir walked to the barber's house holding a large tray on his head. The tray was covered with a clean white piece of embroidered linen. The young boy knew that all the neighbors were watching him from behind the curtains, so he walked very slowly toward the barber's door and gently tapped on the knocker. The barber opened the door and looked sternly at Samir and his tray. Slowly Samir unfolded the cloth. Underneath was a huge round loaf of bread, beautifully decorated with sesame seeds. It could have fed not only the barber's wife but the entire neighborhood. Samir had baked it himself with only a little guidance from his uncle. He was proud to have cooked it to perfection. The barber began to smile and invited Samir in.

HOW THE TORTOISE WON RESPECT
Gcina Mhlophe
A STORY FROM SOUTH AFRICA

In those days, Lion was king, and every single animal respected him. He was mighty and strong and did not have to talk too loudly, for his word was law and that was that. But the animals had a problem. They did not have a place of their own where they could grow food, and they were not yet such good hunters. So they had to go to the gardens of human beings, to steal whatever vegetables they liked. This was often very dangerous, because if they were caught, they ended up in someone's stewpot! In fact, this happened far too often, until one day King Lion could stand it no longer. So he called a big meeting of all his subjects. He told them it was time they all moved to another place where there were no human beings, where they could plant their own food and live a more respectable life.

"*Elethu! Elethu!* We all agree!" was the response from every animal.

Cheetah was sent to go and steal some tools from the humans, which he did with pleasure. Well-known trickster Rabbit was only too happy to go and steal some seeds for his king. All the animals then set off to find a new place where they could grow their own food. The fast-moving animals led the way. In the middle were the king and other big animals like Buffalo, Elephant, and Giraffe. At the back were the slow-moving animals like

Chameleon and Tortoise. The sun was hot and the journey was long. But at last, Cheetah shouted at the top of his voice, "O King, we have found a place. It looks very fertile and there is a lake where we can drink water!"

"But are there any human beings in sight?" was the question from Lion.

"No, not one," replied Cheetah.

The animals worked very hard in the following days, tilling the land and planting their seeds, and soon enough the rains came. In time the garden yielded delicious carrots, pumpkins, cabbages, and sweet potatoes. The animals had a great time eating their food, drinking at the lake, and enjoying glorious sunsets, without any humans to chase or kill them.

Then, one day, Zebra woke up very early with his best friend, Ostrich. They were extremely hungry so they set off for the garden. But when they got there, they found that all the food had gone: not a blade of grass, not a leaf of cabbage was left! Even the lake was almost empty. Someone or something had come in the middle of the night and cleaned up everything. Suddenly, a shadow seemed to fall across the sun, and the sky went dark. When Zebra and Ostrich looked up, they saw a huge mountain of an animal. It was like ten elephants put together. Its skin was moist, grayish brown, and smelly. Its eyes were huge and green and slimy. Its nostrils were like two big caves with hot air coming out of them. Its mouth was the biggest cave of all, full of sharp gray teeth. Zebra tried to be brave, and so he asked this monster who he was and what he wanted.

"I AM GONQONGQO!!!" bellowed the monster, "THE ONE WHO SWALLOWS BUFFALOS ALIVE, HORNS AND ALL. WHO ARE YOU, LITTLE ZEBRA, TO ASK ME SUCH STUPID QUESTIONS?"

Terrified, Zebra and Ostrich rushed off to tell everyone what they had seen and heard. The other animals were frightened, but Lion, their king, said he would deal with Gongqongqo. He said no one should be fearful. Lion's muscles were shining, his tail was up in the air, and his golden mane looked proud as the morning sun danced on it.

But when he arrived in the garden and saw how very large this monster was, he knew he did not stand a chance of winning a fight. He decided to roar as loudly as he could, to scare the monster off.

"Who do you think you are, coming into my kingdom and stealing all the food my subjects have worked so hard for? Get away from here and never come back!" roared the king of the jungle.

Gongqongqo opened his monstrous mouth and answered, "I AM GONGQONGQO! HE WHO SWALLOWS BUFFALOS ALIVE, HORNS AND ALL! AS FOR YOU, LITTLE CAT, I WILL HAVE YOU FOR A SNACK!"

King Lion's tail disappeared between his legs, and he ran as fast as he could back to his subjects to tell them it was time to move to a new place, for this monster was far worse even than human beings.

"*Elethu!* We all agree!" was the response, Buffalo shouting loudest of them all. But Tortoise had other ideas. She declared that she was going to deal with the monster her own way. The other animals just laughed at her, saying that she was far too small, and crazy even to think she could face up

to such a creature. Lion told everyone to shut up, and he listened to what Tortoise had to say. Then he prepared a sharp ax for her and gave it to her to hide under her shell. He wished her luck.

Tortoise set off at a slow pace to face Gongqongqo. She looked tiny as she stood in front of the huge monster. But she bravely shouted at the top of her voice, "*Heyi wena*, who do you think you are? Do you think we are scared of you? No, we are not. Also, I must tell you, you are ugly, and furthermore, you smell! So get away from here, get away!"

The monster couldn't believe what he was hearing. "I AM GONGQONGQO I TELL YOU, AND I DON'T PLAN TO GO ANYWHERE. INSTEAD, I WILL TAKE YOU, TINY TORTOISE, TOSS YOU UNDER MY TONGUE, AND FORGET ALL ABOUT YOU."

And sure enough, his long, slimy, mustardy-colored tongue came out and "*Lwabi!*" Tortoise disappeared inside that mouth!

Then, quick as a flash, Tortoise took out the sharp little ax from under

her shell and started to chop at the monster's tongue. Chop, chop, chop. The monster thought he was getting a headache and groaned loudly. What in the world was going on? What was that dumb little tortoise up to, he wondered, shaking his head violently. But Tortoise did not stop. She continued to chop away at the tongue until it fell off, and then she chopped her way across the neck. Gongqongqo made loud, thunderous noises, scaring the countryside and forest for miles around. Finally, it happened. Gongqongqo fell down dead.

The smiling Tortoise climbed out of a gate she had opened on the side of his neck, and, holding high the little ax, she called out, "It is I. It is I, little Tortoise. I killed Gongqongqo!"

All the other animals came out of their hiding-places and cheered for the brave Tortoise, calling her the cleverest of them all. King Lion declared her the most respectable citizen in his kingdom—after him of course!

Coso cosi cosi iyaphela.

THE ABOUL FAMILY

Hassan Erraji

A STORY FROM MOROCCO

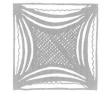

Mr. and Mrs. Aboul lived in a tiny hamlet, right at the top of the mountain of Adrar, close to the western Sahara.

They were poor and humble, even by local standards, and they found it hard to survive. There was hardly ever enough food in their house. A couple of dates and half a glass of goat's milk was their staple diet. They had no land of their own in which to grow vegetables, fruit, or other produce. Their only animals were two goats and one single she-camel. Nevertheless, they were happy, contented with what little they had. Their only regret was that they had no children.

Down in the valley, a big market called the "souk" took place every Monday. Large crowds of Bedouins went to it. Some of the Bedouins were nomads, traveling from place to place with their camels. Some lived in one place, like Mr. and Mrs. Aboul. They all took their produce and possessions to the souk to sell so they had money to buy whatever their families needed. Some of them preferred to barter. They exchanged eggs for a packet of sugar, a lump of cheese for some tomatoes, two or three sheep for a young calf, a pot of honey for a packet of coffee, a bottle of olive oil for a can of soda, a bag of wool for a shirt, and so on and so forth.

Often, Mr. Aboul used to walk happily down the mountain to the market, singing and talking to his faithful companion, his camel. He had heard from his father, and maintained it as a valuable truth, that camels travel smooth and fast to the sound of music.

But Mr. Aboul did not always take his camel. Sometimes he traveled light, so that he could walk through neighboring villages to pass the time of day with old friends.

Sometimes he would set out very early, when the way was deserted, to surprise the occasional fox, hare, snake, or gazelle that was lurking around. He wondered whether it was wise to take these slippery, winding paths through bushes all by himself. Yes, he would convince himself, the thrill made it worthwhile.

Mr. Aboul was going to the souk one day when he suddenly heard a strange, frightening noise. "What is it?" he muttered, speeding up to get away from it. The noise only grew louder and closer. He started running faster and faster, but the ghostly sound, loud and threatening, followed him just as fast. Soon his whole body was shaking and his face was dripping with cold sweat. His hair stood up hard and firm, like nails growing all over his head. Every now and then, he took his courage in his hands and cast a glance backward, but he couldn't see anybody or anything. With his knees trembling and his lips tight-knit, he imagined all kinds of horrible scenes.

At once, he found himself galloping down the narrow pathways, through dangerous terrain and knife-sharp rocks, wishing he could fly. By the time he reached the first oasis on the way to the market, Mr. Aboul couldn't take any more. He fell to the ground among the palm trees. As he fell, the clay pitcher that he was carrying on his back was crushed against a stone, and immediately the strange noise stopped. Only then did Mr. Aboul realize that the sinister sound that had given him such a hard time was only the wind blowing into his pitcher.

As he overcame his panic, Mr. Aboul began to laugh. He laughed and laughed and laughed again.

After that, the thought of his ordeal often made Mr. Aboul chuckle, and on his way to and from the souk he regularly paused and sat among the

same bunch of palm trees, as if to relive the experience.

One day, as he was having a rest in the shade of these trees on his way back from the souk, Mr. Aboul fell asleep. When he woke up, the sun was nearly down. Reluctantly he stood up, shook off sand from his jellaba, yawned lazily, and rubbed his eyes a few times to wake himself up.

Over by the farthest palm tree, something caught his eye: it looked like a pitcher, half buried under the sand. Mr. Aboul hesitated for a while, then decided to check. When he eventually dug it out, it seemed exactly like the pitcher that he had broken in that mad rush a few months before. But this one was intact and felt heavy. Although it was getting late, Mr. Aboul couldn't resist opening it at once. He took the lid off and looked in amazement at what was inside: the pitcher was full to the brim with gold coins.

"How incredible!" he exclaimed. "I've never even touched a gold coin in my life!" He pinched himself a couple of times to make sure he wasn't dreaming. He couldn't believe his luck.

Mr. Aboul's joy was overwhelming. It was too strong to keep to himself.

So back home he ran, losing a shoe on the way, knocking one of his best friends over, ignoring his welcoming camel at the doorway, and smashing the only clay pan in the house as he rushed into the kitchen looking for his wife. When Mrs. Aboul heard what had happened, she shared Mr. Aboul's excitement. That night, they didn't sleep a wink. But, because they didn't have a candle to light, they had to wait for daylight the next morning before they could fully appreciate their newly found fortune.

In the morning, Mrs. Aboul made sure the door was properly locked. She poured a few handfuls of cold water on her eyes and face and then emptied the coins onto the table. Neither she nor Mr. Aboul was sure what to do next. They just kept smiling at each other, holding hands in silence, swaying from

side to side. They felt happy, very happy, for at that point they had no idea that their newly acquired wealth would also bring them a lot of problems and worry.

Soon enough, they heard a noise. It was the sound of footsteps outside. Suddenly they felt very worried. What if the neighbors found out? They might become jealous and unfriendly.

Quickly Mr. and Mrs. Aboul went out to the back of their house, dug a hole under the fig tree that grew there, buried the precious pitcher, cleaned themselves up, and pretended to be enjoying the sunshine, looking over the bush into the valley.

"Good morning, folks," shouted a voice at the front door. It turned out to be Sidi, one of their neighbors coming to visit.

"Good morning, Sidi," answered Mr. and Mrs. Aboul in unison.

"How are you today?" asked Sidi. "You are rather late getting up. Usually you get up early, earlier than the birds, normally."

"Oh," replied Mr. Aboul nonchalantly, "it's just one of those days, you know, when you wake up and find your head weighing a ton. Change of season, no doubt. Anyway, sit down for a cup of tea. And how is Fatma, your beloved wife?"

"Not too bad, thanks," said Sidi. "She also woke up with a bad headache and decided to go back to sleep. So I thought I would come over to say hello. Isn't that nice?"

"Yes, yes," said Mrs. Aboul impatiently. "We always enjoy your visits and conversation, Sidi."

Eventually, Sidi said he must go because he thought he could hear Fatma calling. "See you later," he said, and disappeared.

"You know," said Mrs. Aboul as soon as Sidi had gone, "nobody in the village will believe our story about this pitcher, no matter how hard we try to convince them. Furthermore, jealousy will certainly turn them against us. They will report us to the authorities and then we'll be in big trouble. So let's start packing up right now. Then at midnight sharp, when everyone is asleep, we'll load our camel and disappear."

"Yes, sweetheart," agreed Mr. Aboul. "Excellent idea."

By dawn the following day, Mr. and Mrs. Aboul and their faithful camel had already crossed most of the region where anyone might know them.

Three weeks later they arrived in the city of Tiznit. But the people of Tiznit were not welcoming. Mr. and Mrs. Aboul realized that Bedouins must be a strange sight in the city. People were staring at them because they had a camel and looked different from everyone else. Mr. and Mrs. Aboul did not know what to do next. They had left their home in the village, but their problems did not seem to be over.

With deep regret and with hot tears in their eyes, they decided that if they were going to disguise their Bedouin origins, they would have to sell their beloved camel. And if they did not disguise their origins, the people of this neat and rather snobbish little city might become suspicious of them, find out about their fortune, and accuse them of stealing.

Sadly, Mr. and Mrs. Aboul sold their camel and bought different clothes. They used some of the gold coins to buy themselves a house and a jewelry shop, and they embarked on their new way of life, keeping themselves to themselves.

The new business prospered surprisingly well. Even so, Mr. and Mrs. Aboul were not happy. Money brought them many new things that they had never dreamed of, but it did not bring them peace of mind, and they remained uneasy with their wealth until, one day, they had a wonderful idea.

In the city of Tiznit, there were many homeless children. They were children without parents, without anyone to look after them. It made Mr. and Mrs. Aboul sad. It was not like their Bedouin village where everyone took care of each other. Mr. and Mrs. Aboul decided they would help the children by building them a big, new modern home. When the children moved in, a few months later, the Abouls gave them as much love, care, and education as if they had been their own.

And that is how Mr. and Mrs. Aboul turned out to have the largest family in Tiznit and to be two of the most highly regarded and respected people in

the whole of the region of Adrar. Soon, they felt so much at home that they no longer minded if people knew their Bedouin origins. They even managed to trace their faithful camel and buy her back, much to the delight of their foster-children.

In time, the children grew up and became independent. But they never forgot the great kindness of their foster-parents.

TWO BROTHERS
Inno Sorsy

A STORY FROM WEST AFRICA

(O)nce there was a very rich cocoa farmer who had two sons. He loved them very much. When the time came for him to die, he called his sons to him. He gave all his lands and all his riches to his eldest son. "I also give what is most precious to me: your little brother. Look after him as I have looked after you." After these words, the old man went to join his ancestors.

As soon as the funeral and forty days of mourning were over, a great change came over the Elder Brother. He took to ordering Little Brother around, and instead of looking after him, he made him do the housework, the shopping, and the cooking. Was this what the old man, their father, had asked?

Imagine yourself in Little Brother's position. Wouldn't you cry as he did? Wouldn't you think that life wasn't fair? Wouldn't you miss your father very much?

Well, Little Brother was so unhappy that he didn't eat or sleep at all well; and one night, as he lay on his sleeping mat thinking about how his Elder Brother had changed into a monster, he heard a small noise. He lay very still and listened very hard. There it was again, a small scratching noise. He lifted his head quietly. Sitting on a sack of rice at the foot of Elder Brother's

bed, was a mouse. As he watched he saw this tiny mouse jump from the sack of rice onto Elder Brother's bed. The mouse lifted its whiskers up toward the ceiling, where a basket of peanuts was hanging. Then, gathering all its forces, and with a mighty effort, the mouse leaped straight upward and landed on the rim of the basket.

Little Brother thought he was dreaming. How could a tiny mouse like that jump so high? He watched the mouse pick up one, two, three peanuts, put them in its mouth, jump back down onto Elder Brother's bed, jump back down onto the sack of rice, onto the floor, and disappear under the bed.

I must tell all the people about this, thought Little Brother. It is a very important lesson for everyone. You don't have to be big or rich or anything to do extraordinary things. All you need is determination.

At the crack of dawn he was up, washed and dressed, and on his way to the market.

Now, the market people were used to seeing Little Brother doing the shopping, and they laughed at him behind his back. "Look at him! He's little more than a beggar. His brother is rich and important, but he is only good for shopping and cleaning."

So, do you think they believed his story about the mouse? Of course not.

"He is jealous of his brother, and he wants some attention. That is why he makes up these stories of the mighty flying mouse." I'm afraid this is the kind of thing people said about Little Brother, and when Elder Brother heard about this, he was very angry indeed.

"You are bringing shame on our family name. Everyone is laughing at us. Please don't make up any more of your ridiculous tales, Little Brother."

Little Brother was very upset and hurt that nobody believed his story.

"My own brother treats me like a servant, and people laugh at me even though I tell them what is true and important. I will go away to the forest, and I will learn some more from the forest animals. The mouse has taught me a lesson, and maybe other animals have lessons to teach me." He was very sad to leave his village, but he was determined, just like the mouse.

Not long after Little Brother went to live in the forest, Elder Brother lay awake one night worrying about his cocoa farms when he heard a small noise, a small scratching noise. He raised his head and saw a mouse leaping for the peanuts just as Little Brother had said. Elder Brother couldn't believe his eyes. The next morning, when he met his friends, the rich young men of the village, he told them the story of the mouse.

"Oh!" they said. "This is amazing! How high did this mouse jump? This is a very important discovery. Thank you, Elder Brother, for sharing your great knowledge with us."

Soon, the whole village was talking about Elder Brother and his flying mouse. People came to Elder Brother to ask his advice about all their problems, and everyone agreed that he was a very wise and observant man. Nobody remembered that Little Brother had told the same story. That is why we say, "A poor man's word is nothing, but a rich man's word is gold."

And what about Little Brother? He was still living in the forest with the animals. The animals taught him a lot. They taught him their language and other secrets too.

One day, the animals came to Little Brother with some very bad news. They told him that the people of his village were in desperate trouble.

The animals were right. Little Brother's village had been struck by illness. First the children and then the elders got a very high fever. All the medicine priests and priestesses tried to cure the fever, but it was too strong. The market was silent and empty. Even the children had stopped laughing and playing. How do you cure such a high and strong fever?

Little Brother did not waste time. He gathered together some of the special leaves of the forest which the animals had taught him about, and he hurried to help his people. When he got to the village, he boiled the fever leaves and gave them to those who were sick. In a few days, they began to recover and soon they were well again. You could hear the children playing

once more and the market people gossiping over their goods: "That Little Brother is something special. He is a great healer. He is a very important man."

Little Brother just smiled when he heard this kind of thing.

"I learned this lesson long ago," he said. "You don't have to be rich to do important things. You need determination like the mouse, and you need to find what you are good at. Each one of us has something special that is useful for everyone."

Do you know what you have that is special? No? Well, what are you waiting for? Find it!

TIYOTIYO
Charles Mungoshi

A STORY FROM ZIMBABWE

Long, long ago there was a village where the people didn't know about grain. They lived on meat from wild animals and birds, wild fruit, tree bark, and roots.

Now in this village, there lived a young man named Gano, and his aged grandfather, Muto. Gano was lame. His leg was bent at the knee so he could not stretch it. This meant that he couldn't go hunting with the other young men of the village. As for Old Muto, he was so old that all he could do was wake up in the morning and sit against the wall of his hut in the sun. So, for most days of the week, Gano and his grandfather would go hungry.

Because he couldn't go hunting, Gano was always alone. Early in the morning he would go into the bush. All day he would search for wild fruits or locusts, which he would take back to his grandfather in the evening. There were also birds' eggs. But Gano couldn't stand robbing birds of their eggs. Whenever he looked at nestlings, he thought that they looked as unprotected as he was.

Then one day, when he was out in the bush, Gano heard the urgent whirring of a bird in swift flight. The bird burst into the open. Then it fell with a flurry of wings a few steps from where Gano was standing. The bird

rose up, flew for a few beats of its wings, fell again, rose again and then fell once more without rising. Gano rushed to it and picked it up. He noticed that one of its legs was broken. Then he heard the blood-curdling howling and barking of dogs in pursuit. Gano clutched the bird to his breast and struggled up the low-hanging branches of a muonde tree. The dogs passed by, but their owner saw him. It was Kondo, the leader of the village hunters. If Gano hated any of the young men in the village, it was Kondo he hated the most. Kondo was the one who was always most unkind to him.

"Get down here and give me the bird!" Kondo barked at Gano.

"What bird are you talking about?" snapped Gano.

Kondo was already fixing an arrow to his bow. "You want me to bring you down with my arrow?"

"Go ahead and shoot me!" said Gano.

Kondo was about to release his arrow when, just at that moment, Old Muto's friend, Old Marumba, passed by. Old Marumba was in the bush searching for medicine herbs and he had heard the dogs barking.

"Let him keep the bird, Kondo. You can always hunt for another one," Old Marumba said.

For Kondo, that wasn't the point. He didn't want to give a bird—or anything for that matter—to Gano. Nonetheless, he turned and left.

"Thank you," Gano said to Old Marumba as he got down from the tree.

They made their way home together, and as they walked, Gano told Old Marumba what had been on his mind for a long time. He wanted to leave the village.

"Where would you go?" Old Maruma asked.

"I don't know. There must be somewhere. I just think I don't belong here any more. Even my grandfather despises me because I can't go hunting. I'm no use to anybody."

"Everyone is of some use to everyone," the old man said quietly. He couldn't think of anything that would really comfort Gano. He wished he were good at words.

At home, Gano set about treating the bird's broken leg. After cleaning the

wound with a herb that killed maggots, he tied the leg between two slats of bamboo. As the days went by, he found himself talking to the bird more and more, more than to his grandfather or any other human being. It was a strange bird. He had never seen one like it before. He would speak to it almost every day. "Where do you come from, stranger? What is it like where you come from? Will you take me there one day?"

Then, one day, the bird said, "*Tiyotiyo.*"

Gano looked at it in amazement. He had perfectly understood the bird. It had said, "Wait a little bit longer." Gano began to realize that, without knowing it, while he had been living with the bird, talking to it, feeding it, and treating its leg, he had been learning its language! There weren't many words in the language. Just that one word: *tiyotiyo*. Yet the bird could say so many things with it!

Sure enough, Gano didn't have long to wait. One day, the hunters of the village, led by Kondo, went out hunting. Three weeks later they had still not returned. The longest time the hunters had stayed in the bush before was two weeks. There was no news of them. Not even a single dog had returned to alert people to what might have happened. Every day Gano woke up to hear the women of the village singing:

"The sun comes up
And not a breath of wind
To bring the news of my husband.
The sun goes down
And not a shadow on the horizon
To say my son is coming home.
Another sun comes up
Yet the bush remains deathly still."

Gano heard the women singing, but he could not help them.

Then one day, when the bird had completely healed, it led him into the nearby hills. There it showed him a strange grass that bore little brown grains.

"*Tiyotiyo*," said the bird. And Gano understood that he had to gather the grain.

"*Tiyotiyo*," the bird said again when Gano had gathered a knee-high pile onto a flat rock. This time the bird was telling him to take two rocks, a small one and a large one, and grind the grain between the rocks into flour. As Gano ground, the bird made many trips to a nearby river, fetching water in its beak. When Gano was finished, there was enough water to fill six ostrich eggshells.

"*Tiyotiyo*," the bird said. Gano understood that he was to mix the water with the flour into a paste. When he had done this, the bird showed him a hacha fruit tree. Gano collected the hacha and brought them to the rock.

"*Tiyotiyo*," the bird said. Gano peeled the hacha and squeezed them to extract the juice.

"*Tiyotiyo*," the bird said. Gano added the juice to the paste and set this on the rock to dry in the sun.

"*Tiyotiyo*," the bird said, and Gano tried the paste which had now dried into a hard cake. It tasted good. Now Gano knew that he didn't have to worry about being unable to hunt. He had become the first man in the hunters' village to make food from the seeds of grass.

"*Tiyotiyo*," the bird said. Gano was not to tell anyone yet: first they had to go on a long journey.

So they traveled.

And traveled and traveled and traveled, and all the way, the bird would sing to Gano so that he wouldn't feel tired.

"It's not a long way,
It doesn't take a day,
Coming is going
Going is coming.
Now I've reached the end
Already I'm coming back
I have seen all there is
And now this is only a story."

They traveled until they reached a place that was known as Deadman's Cave. The mouth of the cave was filled with rocks and rubble.

"*Tiyotiyo*," the bird said, and Gano began to move the rubble. It took all his strength to push aside the rocks. In the cave behind were Kondo and the hunters and all their dogs.

How glad they were to see Gano! The hunters told him how a strange bird had lured them into the cave and how the entrance had fallen in behind them, trapping them inside.

"*Tiyotiyo*," said Gano's bird. Gano understood. He gave the men the cakes he had made, and the men thanked Gano when they had eaten.

"*Tiyotiyo.*" Gano was startled. This time, the sound he had heard was strange. It was not the voice of the bird he knew. He saw that it was another bird.

"*Tiyotiyo.*" Now it was Gano's friend who was speaking, saying that it was her mate who had lured the hunters into the cave in order to teach them a lesson.

"*Tiyotiyo, tiyotiyo,*" the two birds said, and Gano told the hunters to follow him. The birds led them to a plain where strange grass grew. It was the kind of grass that had given Gano the grain to make the cakes. Gano then asked Kondo to go back home to bring all their people to this plain.

And that is how the people of the hunters' village learned to grow grain crops. They also promised to give a home to the two birds that had helped them. And although some tribes today kill and eat them, those first growers of grain took the birds, which were pigeons, as their greatly honored friends.

MY GODFATHER
Sousa Jamba
A STORY FROM ANGOLA

I am going to tell you about my life. My name is Chisola, which means love. Where I come from all names have meaning. I am ten years old and I have a young brother, Emmanuel, who is four. I like him very much. War forced us to leave our village called Zunda. My father was a teacher at Zunda, where I was born. We were all very happy. I liked going with my father deep into the forest looking for yellow flowers, which my mother put in a tin in our house. Sometimes we went into the forest looking for leaves, which my mother would rub into the mud floor of our house. The leaves made the house smell like perfume.

Whenever I went into the forest, the thought of lions frightened me. There were many stories of lions that had attacked men who had wandered into the forest. I should not have worried because my father had a gun. We never saw a lion, but one day we heard an elephant which was screaming. The screaming elephant frightened me so much that I held on to my father. When the elephant came toward us my father fired into the air. The man from the Wildlife Department never allowed the people in our village to shoot at elephants. He said too many had already been shot for their ivory. The elephant went away. I felt sad because I like elephants. They used to come very near to our village and were friendly animals, although when they were hungry, they tore the trees because they like to eat the bark. My father told me that in India little boys could ride elephants. Sometimes I would sit imagining that I had gone to India and was riding an elephant.

At special times, such as Christmas, a man from the Wildlife Department, who looked after all the animals in our area, came in a white Land Rover and allowed the villagers to shoot an elephant and sell the meat. My mother, like most people in the area, used to dry the meat in the sun. We children usually had to look after the meat while it was drying because there were birds which would suddenly come down and seize pieces of it. They were large, clever black birds and they loved to eat the meat.

Every evening my father would switch on the radio and listen to the news. There was war in our country. There were people trying to overthrow the government. My mother hoped the war would not come to where we lived. Every evening after dinner, we would sit at the table, with the kerosene lamp in the middle, and my father would lead us in prayer. Sometimes he

would tell us stories from the Bible. I liked the story about Moses and how he let open the Red Sea with his stick. I prayed hard, hoping that war would not come to our area because I liked my school and I liked playing soccer with all my friends. I also liked Tiger, the little dog that Mr. Minga, my god-father, had given me on my eighth birthday.

Mr. Minga was a teacher at the school in the next village. I was very lucky to have him as a godfather. I liked him very much because he always brought me a pencil whenever he came to our house. Sometimes he brought me an exercise book. He also allowed me to try on his thick glasses. My mother always told me never to ask to try on the glasses because I could break them, but Mr. Minga would often say, "Come over here, Chisola, put them on. I know you want to." Mr. Minga's wife, Aunt Bertha, was very thin and quiet. She never spoke. Every Christmas she would help organize a play at the local church. Mr. Minga and Aunt Bertha had a child, a girl called Ruth who was three. Sometimes when Mr. Minga and his wife came to our house I had to look after Ruth. Emmanuel and I liked playing with her. One day, she put her hand into Tiger's mouth. I had to run to pull it out.

There was more news of fighting in the cities. Whenever other elders came to visit my father they told him how the bombs had burned so many houses. I felt scared. My father told me not to worry because the war would soon be over. One day I found my mother sitting at the table. The Bible was open in her hands. She had tears in her eyes but she would not tell me why she was sad.

Then one afternoon, we heard a loud explosion from the village where Mr. Minga lived. We were at school. My father was very calm as he told everyone to go home. I was frightened. I wished there was something I could do. I wished I could protect everyone. Late that afternoon, a herd of elephants went past our village running very fast. We had never seen any-thing like that.

My father came and said, "Chisola, you have to pack your clothes. We are going away." I tried to ask my father what was going on, but he told me to get on with the packing. I packed the few clothes I had in a bag and went

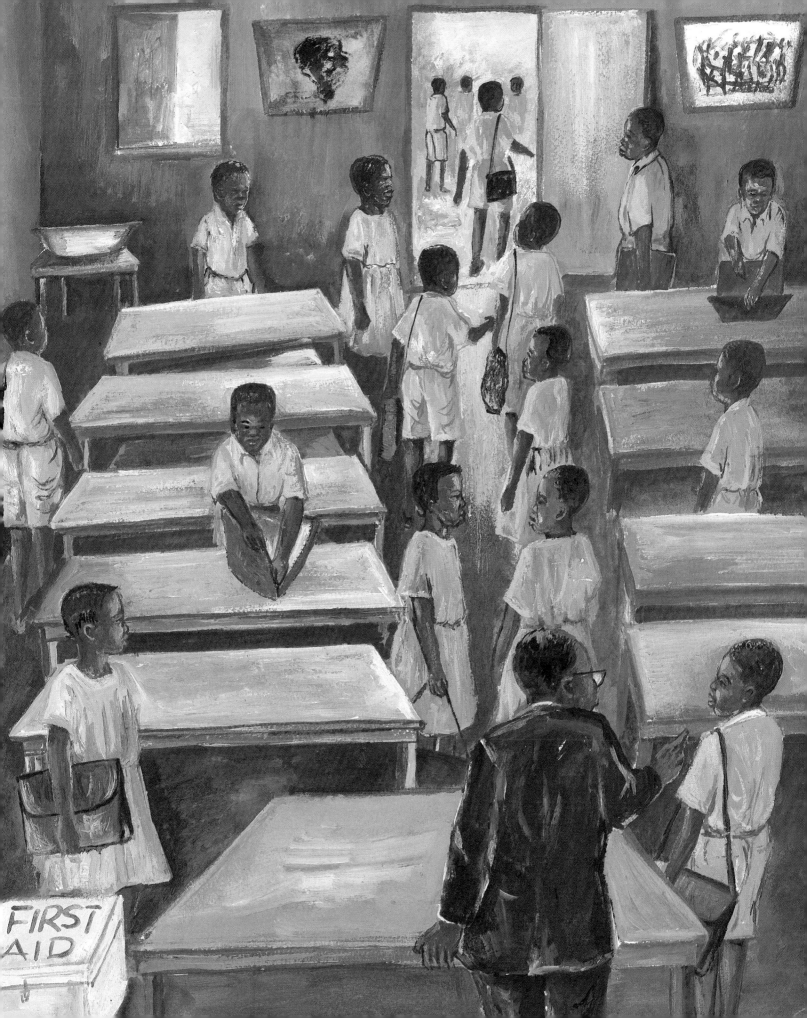

FIRST
AID

into the sitting room. I was very anxious. I felt there was so much Father was not telling me. I thought of my friends and the games we used to play. I thought of our school and how the villagers had worked so hard to build it. I thought of the elephants that used to go past our village.

That night, my father listened to the radio again and kept shaking his head. Mr. Lunkondo, a friend of my fathers who lived near Mr. Minga, arrived at our house. He was sweating and asked for water as soon as he stepped inside. Then he said to my father that he needed to say something to him in secret. They went out in the dark. When they returned, my father was looking worried. He said, "Mr. Minga is missing. He disappeared this afternoon. I think we have to leave at once."

We walked all night. My father and mother took turns carrying Emmanuel. It was dark and silent. Sometimes we heard strange, sharp noises coming from the insects. Tiger came along with us. He was very quiet. I was tired and frightened, but I did not say anything. I just kept listening to the adults as they talked about the war. They said we would be away for just a few days. I was very sad for Mr. Minga. I kept thinking of Aunt Bertha and Ruth. I wondered what had happened to Mr. Minga. Of all the adults that I knew, he was my best friend.

Early the next morning we came to a village that was near the border of our country. The people there were kind and friendly. They brought us bread, sugar, and eggs. Most of the adults in this village were not strange to us; they had already been to our church in the past. I played with some of the children and felt happy. My father said we were going to stay in this village until it was safe enough to return home.

Three months passed. I thought the war was never going to end. We didn't hear anything of my godfather. Every evening we mentioned him in our prayers. My father kept listening to the news and shaking his head. If the war got worse and that village was affected, he kept saying, we were going to move into the neighboring country.

Then, one afternoon, I could not believe my eyes. I saw Mr. Minga, Aunt Bertha, and Ruth in front of the clinic of the village we were in. Tiger rushed to them, barking happily. I hugged Mr. Minga. He wasn't wearing his glasses. He said he had lost them when he and his family were fleeing from the war.

That evening, after supper, my father asked me to say the prayers. I was surprised. He had never asked me to do so in the presence of visitors. I took a deep breath and thanked God for looking after my godfather.

THE NEW MOON AND THE RAIN HORN

Gaele Sobott-Mogwe

A STORY FROM BOTSWANA

Motlalepula's grandmother was very, very old. When anybody asked her age, Grandmother always said, "I was born many moons ago." Motlalepula's grandmother knew time by the coming and going of the moon. She knew when it was time to plant seeds by looking at the moon and she knew when it was time to harvest. Grandmother would say, "Motlalepula, if you are the first to see the new moon, you must make a wish. Do not make a selfish or nasty wish. Make a wish that will help the Earth and you will be happy."

But Grandmother always saw the new moon first. Sometimes Motlalepula forgot to look at the moon, and Grandmother would say, "I made my wish today." Then Motlalepula would look into the sky and see the thin slice of new moon.

Motlalepula's grandmother loved to tell stories. She told stories about how the first people came onto the Earth. She often talked about the men and women who lived in Africa before Motlalepula. She talked of old ways and she also told stories about giants and witches and wonderful animals. Motlalepula learned writing and reading and mathematics at school, but from her grandmother she learned about the Earth, the stars, and the moon, and the people who came before her.

One day, when Motlalepula was coming home from school, her grandmother called her. "Motlalepula! Put your books inside and come with me."

Motlalepula put her books in the house and followed her grandmother. Grandmother walked very slowly with the help of a walking stick that someone had given her. The handle was carved into the shape of a lion's head. There were other animal shapes cut into the stick, and Motlalepula loved looking at them. There was a rabbit, a crocodile, a monkey, an elephant, and a snake. Grandmother could walk long distances. Motlalepula often went with her after school. Grandmother showed Motlalepula different roots and plants. She taught her the names of the plants and what they could be used for.

"Look," said Grandmother, pointing to where some trees had been cut down. "People have been cutting down the trees for firewood. It is not the right time to cut down these trees and too many have been cut. These people no longer know the ways of nature. When I was young the Chief would tell the people when they could cut certain trees for firewood. Sometimes we were not to touch the trees. People do not know these things today. They will make the rain snake angry and we won't have rain. The seeds will not grow and we will not have a good harvest."

Grandmother had told Motlalepula many stories about the rain snake. The rain snake was frightening. Only people with special rain-making power could climb the hill where the snake lived. Only people with special power could take roots and plants from the hill. The rain snake wouldn't harm rain-makers, but anyone else who dared climb the hill would disappear for ever.

"Motlalepula," said Grandmother. "Today, I am going to take you to the hill where the rain snake lives."

Motlalepula thought of the giants, witches, and wonderful animals that Grandmother had spoken of. She had thought that the rain snake was just a story. Now she began to feel frightened.

"Is the rain snake real, Grandmother?"

Grandmother just laughed, and Motlalepula followed her up the hill. When they got to the top of the hill Grandmother sat on a big rock. She was tired. Motlalepula could see where they lived from the hill. She could see the village and the fields.

"When I was a child, my father taught me the secret of making rain," said Grandmother. "Now I am going to teach you that secret. I will teach you how to call soft, gentle rain that makes plants grow."

Motlalepula listened to everything her grandmother said. Grandmother opened the straw basket she had been carrying over her shoulder. Inside was a bowl and a small horn wrapped in a cloth. There were also some small bottles filled with different-colored powders. Grandmother showed Motlalepula where to dig for roots. She picked some leaves and showed Motlalepula how to crush them into a paste. They mixed the powders and paste together in a bowl. Grandmother put some in the horn. She showed Motlapula how to sprinkle the powder on the earth.

"When the time comes, Motlalepula, this rain horn will be yours. You must look after it. The time will come. You will know what to do."

When Grandmother died some years later, Motlalepula felt sad. She missed her grandmother very much. After school she would come home and study. She put all her energy into working for her exams. She didn't notice that the grass and trees were becoming dry and brown. She didn't notice that the crops were not growing well. There was no rain. Motlalepula still missed her grandmother, but she was too busy to think of the new moon and all that her grandmother had taught her. Motlalepula had to think about her future. She wanted to get a job. She decided to leave the village and go to the city to find work. Before Motlalepula left, her mother gave her the walking stick and straw basket that had belonged to Grandmother.

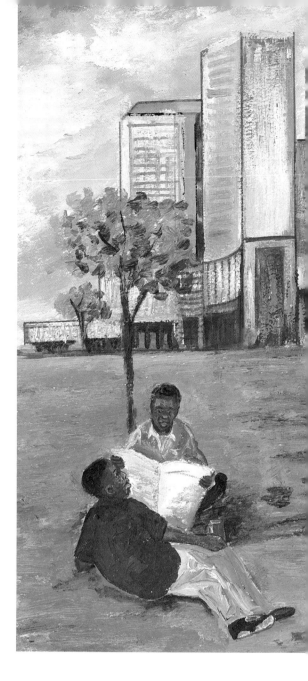

"Here, your grandmother wanted you to have these," she said gently.

Motlapula looked into the straw basket and saw the bowl and horn wrapped in a cloth. Then she packed everything into her suitcase and set off for the city.

When she arrived she was lucky enough to find a job in the city park. She worked in the place where they grew trees and flowers from seeds. She looked after the young trees and flowers, and when they were big enough she gave them to the gardeners to plant in the park. There was plenty of water in the city, and she made sure the plants were well watered and cared for. The people in the city loved to walk under the trees and among the flowers. Motlalepula sent money home to her mother and father to help pay

for her younger brother to go to school. She saved up so one day she could go to university to learn more about trees and flowers. There was a lot to do in the city, and life was busy.

One day, an old man from Motlalepula's village came to her door. "I was a friend of your grandmother's," he said. "I know that she was close to you, so I have come to ask you to help with the rain. We cannot grow anything and the animals are dying."

Motlalepula remembered the old man. She knew that he had been a good friend of her grandmother's so she made him a cup of tea and then went into her bedroom and pulled her suitcase out from under the bed. The walking stick, the straw basket, the bowl, and the horn were inside. She had forgotten about them. She had been so busy in the city that she had not had time to think of the crops and animals. She hadn't thought of rain in the city where there was so much water. She sat there looking at the bowl and the horn for some time. She held the walking stick and looked at the animals carved on it. She thought of her grandmother and all her grandmother had taught her.

"Yes," she said to the old man. "I cannot promise to make rain, but I will try to help you."

The old man was very happy. The two of them caught a bus to the village. It was dusty and hot. When they arrived, Motlalepula left the old man and walked slowly toward the hill where the rain snake lived. She thought about the stories of the rain snake. Her grandmother had told her that only people with the power to make rain could climb the hill. Did she have the power? She was no longer frightened of the rain snake. Using her grandmother's walking stick she slowly climbed up the hill, carrying the straw basket over her shoulder. When she got to the top, Motlalepula dug up some roots and ground them into a powder. She did all the things her grandmother had taught her. She had to work quickly, as the sun was going down. When she had finished she wrapped the horn and the bowl in the cloth and looked out across the fields and the village. As she looked, she noticed a tiny slice of silver moon in the sky. Motlalepula knew it was the new moon and she made a wish. She wished for rain.

When she came down the hill, Motlalepula walked past the place where the trees had been cut down. There was only one tree left. Motlalepula looked at the tree for a long time. Then she had an idea. She would take the seeds from this last tree to her work in the city. She would grow the seeds and look after the young trees. She picked some seed pods and wrapped them in the cloth with the horn and the bowl.

That night, as Motlalepula and her family slept, a soft, gentle rain fell. The rain continued to fall the next morning when Motlalepula caught the bus back to the city. The people of the village were very happy and Motla-lepula too was happy. She looked at the seeds that she had taken from the tree. She knew that she would bring young trees back to the village. She would teach people how to plant and look after the trees like they used to when her grandmother was young, many moons ago.

Editor's Note

The invitation to select these stories gave me one special pleasure. I could ask Kasiya Makaka Phiri and Gcina Mhlophe if they would write down stories I had heard them tell, one at a storytelling festival in Cape Town, the other at a new shopping center in Johannesburg. I very much wanted to experience those stories again, but recapturing an oral story in print is not an easy task. They succeeded superbly.

As I had discovered on my first visit—and it's one reason I love going back—stories are enormously enjoyed and valued in Africa. Since ancient times, they have provided a way of sharing wisdom, wit, and knowledge. When they are told, the listening is loud.

Many contributors—Amoafi Kwapong, Inno Sorsy, and Hassan Erraji among them—are working storytellers and musicians, helping keep Africa's oral traditions alive, bringing to new audiences stories they remember from childhood as well as stories they may have created themselves. Their stories convey the power and magic of live storytelling. Others, like Funmi Osoba, Charles Mungoshi, and Asenath Bole Odaga, are keeping Africa's oral traditions alive in print. Masée Touré is a new, young writer who is both wise and excited about the stories she has inherited and what they can give to others.

The wells of African oral tradition are deep. Now, more than ever before, the world needs the refreshment they offer. But Africa today is a place of huge modern cities as well as traditional villages, dusty roads as well as jungles. I felt it vital to reflect this. The new stories from Eva Dadrian, Gaele Sobott-Mogwe, and Sousa Jamba show Africa is experiencing similar challenges to much of the rest of the world in reconciling traditional and contemporary ways of life. The answers it helps to create are a vital part of a bigger story.

Africa has given me a lot. Compiling this book has been a welcome chance to give something back. I hope, in time, it may reach many of Africa's children. But wherever it travels, I hope it brings greater awareness of the wealth of Africa's talent for stories, showing how stories can help us share our insights into the problems and pleasures of living.

Mary Medlicott

Story and Author Notes

THE RIVER THAT WENT TO THE SKY
Kasiya Makaka Phiri

Born in Zimbabwe to Malawian parents, Kasiya was educated in Malawi, where he later taught in schools and colleges. He is a poet, playwright, and storyteller. He tells new stories and retells old ones first to his three young daughters and then to audiences of all ages. He now lives in Wisconsin, where he is working on a Ph.D. in African literature.

The theme of Kasiya's story is a traditional one, but his tale is also very personal. He says that many things inspired him to write it: "The Limpopo River, a flight over the Sahara, the migration of wildlife on the plains of east Africa, and the great spectacle of the transition from the dry to the wet season."

He sees this collection as "a great support for the evolution of our African culture in these days of rockets, lasers, and bombs."

GLOSSARY
calabash: a tropical tree gourd, the dried skin of which is used for making cups and bowls
tree pangolin: a long-tailed anteater
addax: an antelope with spiraling horns, now quite rare in Africa
jerboa: a desert rat that looks like a miniature kangaroo

GONG GONG
Amoafi Kwapong

Amoafi was born in Ghana and has worked in Africa and Europe as a teacher and performer of African oral traditions. She is currently living in Britain teaching voice studies and African music to young children and working in schools as a professional storyteller.

Gong Gong was inspired by a rhyme in the Twi language of Ghana. Amoafi often tells the story to young children—they love its musical rhythms.

GLOSSARY
Akan (a-KHAN): the Akan people live in eastern and central Ghana
TWI WORDS
nkate (n-KAH-tay): peanuts or groundnuts
kwadu (QUAH-doo): banana
kokosi (koh-KOH-see): coconut
aborobe (ah-bor-RO-beh): pineapple
paya: avocado
akutu (ah-KOO-too): orange
atadwe (ah-TAH-jweh): tigernuts
atea (ah-TAY-ah): cashews
adua (ah-DOO-ah): black-eyed beans
ntaade (n'TAH-day): clothes
ntama (n'TAH-mah): cloth

THE HUNTER AND THE DEER-WOMAN
Funmi Osoba

Funmi is a writer and barrister who originally trained as a film-maker. She divides her time between Britain and Nigeria, where she researched and wrote a book on Benin folktales and legends.

Her story is based on a well-known Yoruba folktale. The Yoruba are a group of people occupying much of the southern belt of west Africa. They have a rich storytelling tradition that can be traced back thousands of years.

Funmi chose to retell this story because "it is not the sort of story that is usually associated with African folklore, which is more famous for its animal fables. It's such a whimsical and beautiful tale."

TWO OF A KIND
Masée Touré

Masée was born in Freetown, Sierra Leone and has had a collection of stories published, despite still being at school in England. She plans to be a professional writer.

She says of *Two of a Kind*: "I have heard the story of the extremely greedy man and the unsatisfied beggar from four different sources—my grandmother, my great-grandmother, my mother, and my aunt. Although the moral issue was always the same, each version of the story was different. There lies the beauty of storytelling in Sierra Leone. Each storyteller is free to add some spice to a story. This is a new retelling entirely from my own imagination, and I would like to share it with young people from all over the globe."

GLOSSARY
Alpha: (AL-fa) a holy man
kaftan: a long sleeved robe
foo foo: mashed yams or bananas
okra: a tropical plant with edible pods
boubou: (BOO-boo) cloth worn wrapped around a woman's head

NO PROBLEM
Asenath Bole Odaga

Asenath was born in Kisumu in Western Kenya, where she still lives. She is one of a small number of professional women writers in her country. She writes in Luo (her mother tongue) and English and has had published over thirty books for children, as well as plays and novels.

Asenath's story is a retelling of a folk narrative of the Luo people, who are the second largest ethnic group in Kenya. The Luos have a rich oral tradition and animals are often used in stories to represent different human characteristics. She says that "the fly who innocently triggers off the events of the story is a humble creature while the fire and rain are powerful elements and the elephant is respected for his huge size. But all the characters are forced to live together and all must recognize each other as being part of the same world. It is for these reasons that I chose this Luo narrative because I wish other children, not only Luo children, to read and enjoy it, and to learn something from the many messages it embodies."

A MOST FAMOUS BAKER
Eva Dadrian

Eva was born in Cairo in Egypt and was bedridden with illness for much of her childhood. Because she couldn't go to school or play with her sisters, she began entertaining herself with stories, and as an adult she still enjoys writing for children.

Of her story she says: "In Egypt bread is basic to any meal. When someone says 'I broke bread with him' it means 'we are friends, we trust each other, we know each other.' Uncle Fathi, the baker of the story, is based on a real person. He was the owner of the bakery where, as a child, I often went with my grandmother. I was fascinated to see how proud that man was to be a baker—proud of his bread and proud of his profession. Despite the long hours and the hard work, he always smiled and had a nice word for every single person who stepped in his bakery."

GLOSSARY
cumin (KOO-min): a spice often used in north African cooking
Hagg: a title given to a Muslim man who has completed the pilgrimage to the holy city of Mecca. In Egypt, Hagg is used in a familiar way for any elderly man.

HOW THE TORTOISE WON RESPECT
Gcina Mhlophe

Gcina is a leading children's writer and performer in South Africa. As well as traveling to Europe, the United States, and Japan for her work, she is also the director of Zanendaba Storytellers in Johannesburg, an organization that is committed to supporting and preserving the art of storytelling in schools.

She says, "This story comes from the Xhosa (HO-sah) people of South Africa. There was an aunt who used to tell this story so well when I was about twelve, thirteen years old. I used to listen to her voice and look at her facial expressions—so real, that before I knew it she had disappeared and in my mind's eye I was in that long ago place. I could see everything. I could even smell the big Gongqongo! When Tortoise had won and everyone cheered for her, I was there cheering loudest.

"The Xhosa language relies a lot on natural sounds. Someone who drinks or swallows big quantities as fast as lightning is imitated as going 'gonqo, gonqo, gonqo.'"

GLOSSARY
elethu (el-LAY-too): We all agree
Gongqongqo (gong-KONG-go): one who swallows people, animals, anything whole!
heyi wena! (HEY-ee WAY-nah): Hey you!
lwabi (LWAH-bee): the slurping sound made by the monster's tongue when the tortoise is scooped up
coso cosi iyaphela (CO-so CO-see ee-yah-PAY-lah): this tale ends here

THE ABOUL FAMILY
Hassan Erraji

Hassan is a musician and composer who also tells stories. He is blind and writes using a braille display computer. He was born in a village about 40 miles from Marrakesh in Morocco but now lives in Wales. One of twelve children, he used to tell and listen to stories with his brothers and sisters: "Often sitting in the dark (no electricity then) or in the moonlight, we would laugh when the stories were funny and huddle together when they were frightening."

Hassan says that his story is based on traditional folktales, although "the jug sounding like a ghost and Mr. Aboul running away from fright—that actually happened to my brother-in-law!" He chose to write it for this collection because "it discourages selfishness and underlines how money doesn't guarantee happiness."

GLOSSARY
souk (sook): the Arabic word for a market or marketplace
Bedouins (BED-wins): people who belong to a wandering Arab tribe that lives in the deserts of the Middle East and north Africa. Some Bedouins form settlements, like the one Mr. and Mrs. Aboul live in at the beginning of the story.
jellaba (jel-LAH-ba): traditional long robe

TWO BROTHERS
Inno Sorsy

Inno was born in Ghana and moved to England after a spell in France working as an actress and singer. She is a trained English and drama teacher and works all over Britain and France as a voice tutor and storyteller. Her favorite African stories are dilemma tales and other stories that explore the moral problems we all face.

The story that Inno has retold for this book is traditional to west Africa. Inno first heard the tale when her grandmother told it to her as a child and she is pleased to be sharing it with new readers and listeners: "I hope this message to explore one's talents and develop one's potential helps to propel this traditional, ancient story into the present and the future."

TIYOTIYO
Charles Mungoshi

Charles is a prize-winning writer who lives in Zimbabwe, where he was born. He writes in Shona (the language of the Shona people who live in eastern Zimbabwe) and English and has had eleven books published including two collections of Shona folktales.

He remembers the tale of *Tiyotiyo* from his childhood: "My story is based on a folktale my grandmother told me about the friendship between a disabled boy and a bird with a broken wing, a friendship that changed the life of a whole village. I'd like to think that in a small way my version of the story also reflects how important it is, especially in these modern times, to respect all living things, including animals, birds, and plants."

GLOSSARY
Tiyotiyo (TEE-yo-TEE-yo): the sound made by baby birds
muonde (moo-ON-day): a wild fig tree
hacha (HA-cha): an edible wild fruit

MY GODFATHER
Sousa Jamba

Sousa was born in Angola, the tenth of eleven children, but at the age of nine he fled the country with his sister when civil war broke out. They escaped to Zambia, where he spent most of his childhood. He returned to Angola ten years later to work as a news reporter before coming to Britain on a scholarship to study. He now lives in London and works as a freelance journalist and novelist.

This is Sousa's first story for children. It is based on his own experience as a child caught up in conflict, conflict that twenty years on has yet to end in Angola.

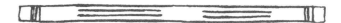

THE NEW MOON AND THE RAIN HORN
Gaele Sobott-Mogwe

Gaele was born and brought up in Australia and is a citizen of Botswana, where she was a university lecturer in English. She is a children's writer with a number of books to her name and is currently studying for a Ph.D. in England. In 1993 she received the Zimbabwe Literary Award for Children's Literature.

The New Moon and the Rain Horn is an original story set in modern Botswana, but the themes of knowledge passed down from generation to generation, and the contrasts of city and village life are characteristic of much of Africa. By ending the story with Motlalepula's plan to replant the destroyed forest, Gaele says she wanted to touch on the often unrecognized efforts of traditional southern African communities to conserve and protect their own environment.